I love you, but...

BEFORE YOU UNLOCK MY PHONE

Dear Reader,

Before I give you my access code, you need to know it's only been a year since what my therapist calls *the great undoing.* It all started when I went back and reread the entire text exchange between my ex and me. Which, by the way, I don't recommend doing.

What you're about to read is the unedited exchange between me and Zoey. Every picture. Every fight. Every thought. Every spelling and grammar error. The painful journey of putting this out into the world has made me realize one thing when it comes to relationships... I'm always the problem.

P.S. The passcode is 061089 - her birthday.

Enjoy,

Green Eyes

YOU DON'T REMEMBER OUR KISS

Wed, April 15 at 11:06am

Apparently we met last night and I got your number?

My friend told me I HAD to text you b/c we had this amazing connection... but I don't remember a thing

Are you serious right now?

Sadly yes

Nothing?

Nothing

If you weren't so funny, I would literally stop responding now...

What about charming? Was I charming too?

Ugh. Yes

You don't remember playing jenga?

No

The guy who farted on us?

No, but I wish

Then you clearly don't remember our kiss...

Ouch. No

How was it?

I'll just say you have soft lips

That's exactly what my priest used to say

I'm kidding. We mostly did butt stuff

That's exit only for me

Let me take you out to dinner and you can recap the evening

Don't think so

Come on

Only if you can describe what I look like

You were that girl in the wheelchair, right? With one arm and no teeth?

Bye!

I refuse to just say you're the most beautiful woman I've ever laid eyes on... b/c that's too easy. Plus you were given your looks, so it's not like you did anything to earn them

So...

You have the ability to make everyone feel special around you, but you're not aware you're doing it. You woke up something in me that I didn't know I had. You truly are very special

I thought you didn't remember anything?

I only remembered meeting you...
and how it made me feel

Where are we eating?

Sparrows. Friday night. 8pm.
I'll pick you up

I'll meet you there

Cautious, I like it

See you then

One more thing

????

I remembered everything.
Reservation's under my name.

CATCHING FEELINGS

Fri, April 17 at 2:22pm

I've never had that long of a dinner before...

Thank you again

I can't stop thinking about you

Oh yeah... what are you thinking about?

For one, how has no guy snatched you up? You're incredible.

Stop it

I can't

Ok, don't stop. More please

I've never been this open with anyone

Me either

It's painful I can't see you for two weeks

I love my family, but I'm not looking forward to this family reunion.

The reason they invented alcohol is because of families... so make sure you stock up

Ha!

Is it cheesy if I want to make plans now, for when you get back?

Yes. Completely.

But I'll allow it

A week from Saturday. Dinner.

This time, I'm picking you up

Done

THE GUATEMALAN

Sun, April 19 at 8:01pm

I just saw this and it made me think of you...

I think I just tinkled in my pants!!! 😂

Tinkled?

Peed

Zoey?

Yes

Sorry, for a second there I thought your grandma was texting for you

LOL!!!

How's the trip going?

Weird

Good weird or bad weird?

Both I guess

Please tell...

My grandma keeps doing mildly racist things to my sister's Guatemalan boyfriend

Like what?

She speaks really slowly to him because she thinks he can't understand English.

Does he speak english?

Yes! He was born here.

Then she keeps asking him and only him, to take out the trash. Fix things around the house. Like he's her day laborer.

Gotta love old people and their privileged views

He should win an award for patience

I'm definitely not that patient

Then my mom told me she has cancer-lite

Oh my god. I'm so sorry

Sorry to ask but what is cancer-lite?

It's cancer

Ok... but it's not a serious form?

No, it's cancer. I'm just annoyed with her and didn't want you to actually feel bad for her.

Then I won't. Congratulations on the cancer. I'm opening an expensive bottle of wine as I type...

She waits till the family reunion to tell everyone. So it can be all about her the whole time we're here

It's complicated

My mom is the same!

Except she would've posted it on facebook and started a gofundme page and then only told us after she raised $1000 dollars to prove the world cares more than we do.

They should meet

I don't think the universe could handle that. It might lead to big bang 2.

They just found it, she's getting a mastectomy

In all seriousness, that sucks. I'm here to talk if you need me.

Despite your tendency toward constant comedy, you have a maturity that I really like

That's very kind of you to say There's too many things I like about you to put in a text...

On that charming note, I need to get back to my racist family

Ahhh, racist-lite family.

I'll harass you later.

IS THE WATER ON

Mon, April 20 at 11:21am

Happy Hitler's birthday!!!!!

Random

Fun fact, it happens once a year

Makes sense

I was just trying to keep up the theme of your trip... racism

I have a book pitch for your grandmother...

Ok

It's called "All the Good Hitler Did"

What good did he do?

We have penicillin, jet engines and ballpoint pens all because of WW2.

I'd rather 80 million people not died

So you're a glass half empty kind of person

HA! How do you sleep at night!!!

Melatonin and whisky

Gotta go. We're leaving for dinner

Send me a pic later

What kind of pic?

Of the bath faucets, please

I can't tell when you're joking??

I'm really into people's faucets.

You never know who's a Kohler family and who isn't.

Okay...

FLIRTING BUILDS TRUST

Mon, April 21 at 1:48pm

Haha!!!

Are we a Kohler family?

I have no idea, I was joking

You're adorable

I meant send me a pic of you!

I'm fucking with you.

Here's the real pic...

Incredibly sexy

Really?

Are you in the tub right now?

Yes

My toes look terrible

Not to me

Can I ask you a personal question?

Sure...

Do you pee in the shower?

Haha!!!

Is that a yes?

I thought you were going to ask me something else

What?

Nothing

Come on

It's silly

This is how we build trust...

I thought you were going to ask me if I wax my...

Upper lip?

LOL! 😭 😭

No, my... you know...

There's no way I was going to ask that

But since we're on the subject...

Yes. It's very smooth.

Noted.

Now that I've been properly embarrassed...

Well, do you?

What?

Pee in the shower with your smooth area?

Yes

Oh, I see

Is that a bad thing?

Do you pee in other people's showers or only your own?

Any shower. I don't discriminate.

Wait, do you pee when you're taking a bath?

Eww. No.

The tub gets an eww no, but shower is a solid yes?

Aren't you basically lying in your own urine right now?

No, I told you I don't pee in the tub.

But isn't that tub the same place you shower? Hence, urine bath?

No, I cleaned it

If it's not inherently gross, then why would you clean it? You let others stand in it when you're done, but you won't lay in it?

It's not the same

I might need some time to think about this

Come on. You don't pee in the shower?

No

Never?

Never.

A very famous person said...There's two types of people in the world, those who pee in the shower and those who lie about it.

Ha! Very funny. But I can proudly say I've never peed in the shower.

But it makes so much sense

There's a drain

Water's flowing. The urge arises...

Some very smart people went out of their way to invent this thing called a toilet. A whole other device just for pee and poop.

Come on, it's all just holes. It all goes to same place.

Please tell me you don't shit in the shower too?

GROSS! No. Never.

That's a huge relief

I'm not a monster

Said the shower pisser

LOL!!!

You said you have a twin sister, right?

Yes

Does she pee in the shower too?

I've never asked.

Can you find out?

Are you conducting a shower pissing twin study?

It's an interesting question, right?

I suppose

You said you guys do most things the other does even if you're not aware you do

I've never even talked about this with anyone till right now

Expand your mind

Ok, I'll ask

Wait, am I a bad person?

Of course not. You're just a serial shower pisser. There's a big difference.

You're impossible!

THERE'S A TEST

Mon, April 21 at 7:19pm

You ready....

I don't know for what, but YES

She pees in the shower

I knew it!

On her feet

Wait, what?!

She saw an interview with madona when she was little and madona pees on her feet in the shower

This story just took a dark turn

Apparently it cures athlete's foot

Is your sister a professional athlete?

What? No. Not even close. She barely has enough energy to walk and get her mail

You don't see the disconnect in her logic?

HAHA! Yes. 

What kind of family am I getting involved with?

None yet. You still have all kinds of tests to pass

Intriguing. Have I passed any so far?

Maybe

Come on

What?

Tell me

You have

But you're not going to tell me?

You have this ability to make me squirm

Is that a bad thing?

No. but that's one of the tests.

Squirming?

Kind of. More like can you hold my interest

Do I?

Yes

You hold mine

I have to text you in private because I have this huge smile plastered across my face every time we text.

Just like that, but I look like a dork and I'm not yellow.

HOW'S THE RACISM

Wed, April 23 at 4:54pm

I got one for you…

Hit me!

Do you share your toothbrush?

With strangers?

Sure….

No. Never.

Good, but I meant with people you know

Of course not. No. Never.

Not surprised. You seem too ridged for such endeavors

Thank you.

Wait, do you?

In past relationships

As a regular thing? Or more like, oh I forgot my toothbrush and in a pinch needed to borrow his?

Both

Look, I don't know where our time together will go… but I want to be clear about one thing…

Yes

I will never share my toothbrush.

Why not?!

My plaque is my business.

But we've already kissed?!

How is that the same?

How is it not?

I know I was drunk the first time we kissed, but did I proceed to clean your gums and teeth with my tongue?

LOL!! No!

That's how it's different

I'm saying it's just as intimate

Perhaps, but one is sexual... the other is hygiene

Not to me

Is this when you tell me it's all holes?

LOL!!! 😂

That seems to be your go to argument

You're ridiculous

How's the racism coming along over there?

I would say mild-to medium spice

How is work?

Blah to good. More blah than good

With the amount we text and talk I can't imagine you get much done

I'm willing to lose my job over it. You're worth it

Stop it, you're making me blush

You stop it

I've been meaning to ask, but did you win the American girl doll account?

Unfortunately, no

Sorry

Don't be. At least I got a free doll out of it

Your ideas were so good! Fuck them

Thank you. Other ones will come along

I know how much you wanted it, I'm sorry

Speaking of, I got to get back to it

What are you working on now?

Vegan cream cheese.

Wow. Sounds yummy.

It's disgusting

HAHA!

THE MIDDLE CHILD

Thu, April 24 at 12:31pm

Hey...

Hey you.

Sorry about last night, my phone died

I assumed so

My sister stole my charger and it was too late to go creeping into her room.

You could've asked the Guatemalan man-servant go get it

LOL! I tried, but it turns out he was sleeping in her bed!

Scandalous!

I felt bad because we were talking about your family when it cut out

There will be plenty of time to talk about my dysfunctional family. Don't you worry.

You were talking about your dad

We can talk about it later

No. tell me

I really want to know about your family

It's important to me

I was saying he left when I was 5 and we never saw him again.

I'm so sorry

It's ok, I'm over it. It's been a long time

But thank you

So it was just you, your mom and your sister and brother?

Yup. And me playing referee between them all

You were the middle child?

Yup. It's exhausting

That why you don't see them much?

Exactly.

But I try to call my mom once a week to check in

That's sweet

Even though we don't get along, she did managed to raise me pretty well considering how full her hands were.

I'd say she did a good job with you

Jury's still out

I want to see a pic

Of my family?

No, of your bath faucets

Touché!

I really want to see them!

Send it!

Shut the front door!

No way!

The far right?

Wait, this can't be real?

HAHAHAHAHA!!!!

Does it make me a bad person if I'm relieved?

Ha! No. not at all. I'm relieved too!

Come on, send me a real one

I don't have any on my phone
I'll have to dig one up

I do have one of me as a little boy,
but it's a little suggestive

Send it!

Ok, but I warned you...

Stop it!

That's me. I was a little terror.

Of course you're a cute kid.

I'M WEARING A DRESS

Fri, April 25 at 3:03pm

So this just happened. In line, buying coffee...

What's this?

Exactly

No, why are you sending me this?

Because America needs to wake up.

No. scratch that, the world

To what?

To women who don't know how to buy jeans that fit right. It's an epidemic

Are you sure this pic was meant for me?

What?! Yes. I'm going to send this to everyone in my contacts

Now I'm worried

Why?

Because I love wearing jeans

Look at me as the red cross for butts, I'm only here to help. There's no judgments, I just show up when tragedy strikes

Please tell me you did not confront that woman?

Damn right I did

On the street?

Yes. Call it a hobby

Now I'm nervous

You have no need to be, you're perfect

Thank you. But I'm nervous about your mental state

Don't be. I'm self-aware-crazy. It's the best kind. Rated number one on trip advisor

LOL!

You certainly keep me on my toes

I never know what you're going to say next

Orange Jello

What?

See, you didn't know

Haha!!!

I think I'll only wear dresses from now on

I've only ever seen you in a dress

And that's how it's going to be

So even if we do decide to have sex at some point...

Yep, I'm wearing a dress and not taking it off

Got it

But for the record you have an amazing body

Thank you

What's your secret?

I see what you're doing here.

Good. I'm glad you can see that I'm just a guy curious about health and fitness.

You're ridiculous

Thank you

I go to the gym and do this cardio class and I've put on 9 pounds of muscle since I've started!

Damn!

Can I tell you something embarrassing?

Please

My favorite thing to do in the class is stare in the mirror when I workout. Then after everyone leaves, I take photos

Ha! Amazing. I'm going to join your class, I need to see this!

It's so vain, but I can't stop

Now, I finally understand why there's all those mirrors in there

Do you want to see?

More than anything.

Oh my god. Amazing!

I know it's ridiculous

It's so many things

But, I love that you do it

I just like to track my progress

So how many pics do you have?

No comment.

Like a few pics a year? Or like I had to call apple to ask what the largest icloud account they offer is?

No comment.

WOW that is a lot!

No comment.

PROUD TO SHARE

Sat, April 26 at 9:56pm

Guess what happened to me today?

Please tell me

I got nominated for teacher of the year at my school!!!

That's amazing!!! CONGRATS!!

Thank you. Thank you

We can celebrate at dinner

That sounds lovely

Really looking forward to seeing you tomorrow

Me too 😋

Okay, I'm getting tired. Sweet dreams

Good night

GUESS WHERE

Tue, April 29 at 12:27pm

Can our date start now?

Definitely not my hair smells like burnt waffles and I'm wearing flats

Don't care. Now please.

What time's dinner?

Reservation's at 8pm. Pick you up at 7:30pm

What's the name of the restaurant?

Don't you want it to be a surprise?

Oh. Ok. I guess

You don't like surprises?

I love them. Just not used to it

Dress as fancy as you want

Ooooh, exciting!!!

See you soon.

BACK OF THE THEATRE

Wed, April 30 at 1:18am

You're so fucking yummy, I can't stand it

Thank you for an amazing night
Sorry, my ass kept changing the song

Haha! I wouldn't have it any other way

What are you doing?

In bed, wishing you were here
What are you doing?

You need to control yourself
I'm teaching you patience... you should thank me

I was pretty controlled. It was you I was worried about

Oh thanks for thinking of me!!!!

You're very welcome. Good thing I got out of the car when I did... Who knows what you would've done to me

I love when you tickled the inside of my hand at dinner

Your skin is so soft

You have very attractive hands

I've never been told that

Will you tickle them again like that next time I see you?

Absolutely

How about tomorrow?

Do you want to see Moana?

I thought you'd never ask.

But I want to warn you, it will be 2 hours of me tickling your hand. Will you be able to handle it?

It will be tough, if I'm being honest

It's ok, we can sit in the back row. I don't want any kids seeing...

Good idea. Sweet dreams.

Wed, April 30 at 9:32am

Good morning!

Good morning!

Did you sleep ok?

Yes. And my sore throat is gone!

You're welcome. I kissed it out of you.

I'm also a part-time shaman

I will feel bad if you get it

Even if I do get it, I don't care. It was worth it

How was the gym?

I don't know... you should ask somebody who made it.

Haha!

You kept me up past my bed time

Was it worth it?

Yes

I'm drinking coffee by the pool, care to join?

I would, but by the time I got ready and got over there you'd be done

I'll sip slowly

So there's a 2:10 Moana, still want to go?

Sounds great!

I'll pick you up

The theatre I looked up is close to you, so I'll pick you up in an hour

You're such a gentleman

It's your turn to be a lady

ALONE WITH A TOY

Thu May 1 at 11:02am

Who knew a G rated movie would lead to X rated sex?

I still feel floaty drunk from it

I don't even know what to say...

Did you not like it?

I think I saw god

HAHA!!! 😳 😆

I knew we had this amazing connection, but that was... just wow.

I think I've been having bad sex my whole life, but as you know, I don't have much experience

And how have you never had an orgasm?

I have, just never in front of anyone

Can I ask you a personal question?

I'll allow it

How do you masturbate?

Hey!

I just had you in my mouth, I don't think I'm crossing any lines

Toys

That's the problem

Don't hate on toys! They're a gift

I love them. But I have this theory, how you masturbate is how you train yourself to cum.

Then we believe that that's the only way we can.

Hmmmm...

You can't cum during sex because you've only trained yourself to do it alone with a toy

Does make sense.

This is going to be hard to hear, but...

You need to give up your toys.

How dare you. I'm the kindergartner teacher here

Just temporarily. Like a time out

I'll consider

Have you ever had an orgasm without a toy?

No

Well then, that's step one

I feel like I'm at an orgasm seminar and I just got a homework assignment

Hey if you want to continue to have orgasmless sex, I support you.

Hmmmmmm...

Maybe we just need to try again

We really do need to give it our all...
I'm thinking tonight?

I mean it's basically for science, so yes

Come over and I'll cook for us

I'd like that

7pm. Come hungry... and come hungry

THE REDUCTION SAUCE

Fri, May 2 at 11:29pm

Thank you so much for such a lovely evening

You're so welcome

Is there anything you can't do?

What do you mean?

You're annoyingly a good cook too

You like?

Love. So good.

I love cooking

It shows

And I can't believe how turned on you get me...

You're so fucking hot it's disgusting

Now all I want is more

Over here it's an all you can eat buffet... so cum any time

LOL! 😀😄😁😆

NOT ON FACEBOOK

Sat, May 3 at 2:38pm

So I just spent an hour on the phone with my sister...

Who was crying her eyes out

Oh no. What happened?!!

Remember how I told you for weeks my mom's been making passive aggressive comments about my niece sleeping in my sister's bed?

Yes. Which I still don't get why she's so weirded out about it?

Apparently my sister went out of town...

And while she was gone my niece slept in their bed with just her dad.

All my friends with kids, do that

This is the normal response, but...

My mom just accused my brother in law of molesting my niece.

To his face?

She said it to my sister, not him

Because they slept in the same bed?

Yes.

Was your mom there that night?

No.

Then how does she know?

She doesn't

Either way, that's terrible.

Most importantly he didn't do it

Thank god.

Then that's a real fucked up thing to say to someone

It is, but that's how my mom rolls

I'm sorry

I think my mom invented gas lighting

It is a skill to be that manipulative

It's this kind of shit that makes me not want to see them

I know but they're your parents

I know, but I'd never be friends with them if I met them today

But that's what family is... A collection of weirdos who help you navigate life

That's a very optimistic outlook

What if they are a collection of weirdos who keep you from living the life you want?

Hmmmm...

I know we just met, but if/when you meet my parents I have a couple of strict rules...

Intriguing, what?

You can't be facebook friends with them.

And you can't give them your phone number or email.

Seriously?

Dead.

But they're your parents?

I know it sounds weird now, but you will thank me

She will end up doing something fucked up to you like what she just did to my sister.

No way 😬 😬

Seriously

I know this may look like a red flag to you, but I promise it's not

Ok...

Can you talk now?

I feel like this has surpassed being a text conversation.

Yes

Calling...

NOT A DILDO

Sun, May 4 at 11:14am

Hi

Hi

Just wanted to say hi and hopefully make you smile

You did

How's your day?

I would say strong, to really strong

Really? Why?

Just landed a new account!

Amazing, CONGRATS! What is it?

I'm not allowed to say

Ok. I understand

But it is secretly killing me

Maybe if you guess it?

Ok...

It's a toy

Is it a dildo?

HAHA!! I did not see that coming.

Very funny!

Thank you. Thank you. (bowing)

Ok. It's plastic. Colorful.

Is it a new toy or an old one?

Old

GI Joe?

No, it's a toy you build with....

Hmmmmmm...

They have a theme park about this toy...

Legos?!

I cannot confirm or deny that.

I understand, but congratulations!!!!! So cool!!!!!

Thank you

We must celebrate. I'm taking you out!

That sounds fun

Wednesday?

I can't. spending time with my niece

So cute tuesday?

Done

Looking forward to it

IT'S IN THE STARS

Mon, May 5 at 10:41pm

I'm sorry I was such a dick

You are?

Yes.

Thank you for saying that

I don't know why I get so irritated

It's ok. You just like things a specific way

I guess I do

Don't get me wrong, I like how organized and efficient you are, but you could loosen up more

I read up on my sign like you said

You did?! So adorable!

Do you see what I was saying now?

You are totally right. It's so me. I'm very... particular

My uptight little Virgo

I also read up on you too

And now the tables have turned!

I can't believe you are a twin in real life, and also a Gemini. It's crazy

It is!

We are going to have to dig in more on that at dinner

Can't wait.

Pick you up tomorrow at 6:30pm

Yay!

TWIN CALLS

Wed, May 7 at 9:01am

I feel terrible that I had to cancel dinner. I'm so sorry

It's ok

Please don't be mad

I'm not. I was just really disappointed

I know. Me too

It's fine. We can celebrate another time

She really needed me. I normally never cancel anything.

I get it

I will make it up to you

How's your day going with your niece?

Good. About to go ice skating

It's melting my heart the image of you ice skating with her

I'm not gonna lie, it's pretty up there on the cute scale

Send me a pic

I think I just melted

She's the cutest.

I'm hitting the ice, call you later

TWO HEADS

Thu, May 8 at 3:22pm

I have a confession...

Ok...

I touched myself thinking about you last night and got there...

So hot

And I did it with no toys!!!

That's a huge first for me!!!!

Amazing! Congrats!

Thank you for all of your encouragement

They say if you can just touch one person in life... or rather get them to touch themselves... you've won.

LOL!!

I've turned a dangerous corner cause now because all I want is more...

I have a big smile on my face and I'm hard.

Both my heads want different things

HAHA!

It's very empowering

And I'm not sure if they can recycle this, but I didn't have the heart to throw it out.

We've been through so much together...

HAHA! That is amazing!!!!!

Sweet dreams.

Good night.

HARRY & SALLY

Sat, May 10 at 4:56pm

Remember how I said I was going to make it up to you for missing dinner....

Yes

SO fucking hot!

But I'm gonna need more than that...

Really?

You look beautiful, but it doesn't quite match the level of disappointment I felt that night

I was looking for something more...

Would you like to come over tonight?

Maybe

Come on!!!

I'm gonna need another pic in order to decide

Seriously?

Yes. Something dirtier

HAHAHAHA!!!!

Pretty dirty huh?

So dirty. Exactly what I wanted.

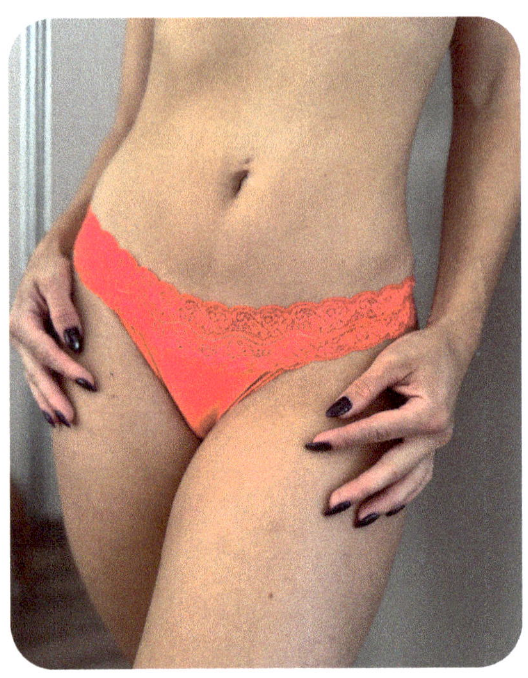

How about now...

Wow. That'll do it

You like?

Too much

What time?

7pm

I thought we could order in and watch a movie?

Perfect. Have you seen "When Harry Met Sally"?

I've never seen it.

You haven't seen it?! It's only the greatest movie of all time!

Can't wait!

Wait, I just remembered that I don't have a TV

My sister's borrowing it

It's okay, I'm sure we can find something to do....

Haha! Yes, please.

SOMEONE TURNED ON THE LIGHTS

Mon, May 12 at 8:14am

I love how turned on you were this morning...

Don't. I'm about to go teach a bunch of 5 year olds.

Sorry

It's ok, I'm at my desk. No one's here yet

I love picturing you at your desk in your sexy little teaching outfit... so hot

Stop it. I'm trying to eat. I'm hungry!

Me too

I can tell

Oh, you'll love this...

Tell me

I was in the teacher's lounge and the gym teacher came in to get coffee and he turned to me and said you look different... there's something different about you, like the light is coming back on

Haha!

Am I glowing or something – sheesh?

Yes, you are

I really like you

I really like you

DOG GUY

Tue, May 13 at 5:40pm

My neighbor just asked if I wanted to go with him to walk his dog

Do you think I should go?

I don't think you should go

You sure?

Like I told you before, you need to set him straight

Would you be a little jealous if I strolled with the neighbor?

No, not at all silly

But like I told you before, he's really giving you the full court press

I see

This dog thing must have worked so many times for him

I'm pretty sure it's his A game

I think you might be right

Trust me, I am.

You're not the jealous type, huh?

I really am not. But if I was I definitely wouldn't be jealous of "dog guy"

I'm glad you're not. I don't like jealousy

I don't either. But I really like you

You just passed another test

Jealousy?

Yep. I hate it

Me too

TOO MANY MOVES

Wed, May 14 at 10:12pm

There's something that keeps coming up in our conversations that I want to make clear....

You seem to be under the impression that all the experience we've been having are all things I've done before

Yes, I have had some of the experiences before, but never and I mean never have they been as right or alive or as amazing as they've been with you

So I just want you to know that even if I've had some of these experiences in the past, everything is very different with you

Thanks for note. I'm mostly just teasing you

Just want you to know that everything we do means a lot to me

And I don't mind all your fancy moves. I like it

Ok, good

And I forgot to tell you...

What?

I really like you

YOU'RE DOING IT WRONG

Thu, May 15 at 3:48pm

I love it when you scratch your fingers hard down my back...

Mmm, I love doing that

I love the sounds you make when you cum

What do I sound like?

You're the only person that knows beside me!

It's these hot sounds of you letting go...

So fucking yummy.

This is my first time sexting

Is that what we're doing?

I think? Right?

Then what are you going to do about it?

I get so hot thinking about you, that I want to tell you all my dirty thoughts..

I love being inside you, staring into your eyes

Mmmm, you're giving me the chills

I love your perfect ass

I want to send you something dirty

Yes please

An appetizer for later...

So fucking hot. Jesus.

It's crazy how turned on I get with you

It's our connection.

I hungry for every inch of you.

You there?

Hello?

Thu, May 15 at 4:17pm

Yes sorry, I just had sex with you.

Did you touch yourself?

Yes. What do you think I mean?

You were getting me all hot with your sexting

We were flirting. Sexting is way different

What you just did is call selfish

Haha! Oh no. I did it wrong?!!! 

No, I think it worked... for you

Oh no!! I'm a selfish sexter!!!

Again, it wasn't sexting... you're just selfish

LOL!

Either way, you're still so yummy, I wish I heard you

I'm still thinking about you. It gives me the chills... it's just ridiculous

And for the record, I've been hard since you sent that pic

That's quite awhile... why don't you take care of that?

It's going to have to wait, I'm stuck in this meeting.

Oh my gosh! I had no idea. Sorry.

Don't be sorry. I'm going to put that picture to good use when I get home.

TWIN PRIVILEGE

Fri, May 16 at 12:39pm

My sister is so annoying!

What happened?

I finally booked our family friend's cabin for a girls weekend

Fun

But she went and invited a bunch of people

That sucks

She never asks what I want, she just assumes it's ok

You should tell her that

No it's fine. I like the people she invited. It's just that some of the girls are better friends with my sister than me. It's annoying

She's always been the more outgoing-popular one.

Everyone always loves her

Maybe you could invite some of your friends too?

She's already friends with all my friends

I know you're sisters and twins and I've never met her but...

Trust me you're the one everyone really wants to be friends with

Sounds like she's trying too hard to be liked

Why would you say that?

I'm just telling you what it sounds like to me

You don't even know her

I know, that's what I said

Let's just talk later

I'm sorry if I offend you.

It's fine. I gotta run

SOME SOUP

Sat, May 17 at 2:09pm

It's annoying you're not on IG

We talked about this

I know, but I feel like I have to tell the world what I'm doing and then I have to repeat it for you later because you didn't see it

This sounds like quite a workload

Have you considered hiring an assistant?

I'm being serious!

I don't want the time we share to be shared with everyone

I think what we do is for us

You and your stupid cute logic.

Were you trying to pick a fight with me?

Maybe...

Are you still mad at me?

No

But I might be on my period and feeling a little crazy

Do you want me to bring you some soup, advil and a heating pad later?

Stop it!!!

What?!

You're freaking me out being all considerate

So, that's a no?

I'm going to the gym to work out all this energy 😋 😜

Don't take too many pictures

KID INSIDE

Sun, May 18 at 6:33pm

I just bought my niece a birthday gift

Soooo cute! What'd you buy her?!

I bought her this little stuffed puppy that comes with it's own little bag that you carry it in. And it has outfits you can dress it in.

And I bought her a book

Adorable! My favorite gift as a kid was books!!! 🤓

What was your favorite book?

Anything by Dr. Seuss

What book did you buy her?

It's about a dog who owns a bookstore.

It's called dog loves books

How cute!!

Apparently, I should've bought you a copy too

Yes, from now on, whatever you buy your 4 year old niece... I want one too

Done

I just wanted to tell you that I really like you

Even with my emotional crying last night?

It made me like you even more

Why?

Because you were being so raw and honest

But what if we end up wanting different things?

That would suck. But we just need to be 100% honest with each other. It will all work out

LET HIM CHOOSE

Fri, May 23 at 12:20pm

Can't wait to see you tonight.

Me too! !!

What are you wearing?

Just got out of the shower, so right now I'm in a little silk robe

Yum

Which panties are you gonna wear?

Which ones do you want me to wear?

The black lace-y ones...

Ok, the black ones then

I'm so turned on just thinking about them

Good. Save it for me

Don't go playing solo before

Yes ma'am

NOT A PEDO

Sat, May 24 at 2:45pm

How's your niece's birthday party?

I'm at the bar with my dad

Is her party at a bar? Very progressive, what kind of drink did she order?

Ha! Pre-partying is the only way to get through a kids birthday party.

We go to Gymboree at 4pm

Oh right, I forgot about Gymboree

What are you doing today?

I'm shopping right now

Wish I was with you

Me too

Especially after last night

Mmmmmm, you just gave me the chills

And for the record, I will buy you a new pair of lace-y black panties

It was worth it... so hot

RIP black panties

I totally thought someone was going to see us

We'll have to go back there

Yes, please

I sneaked a pic

What?! When?!!

During...

What?!

It's not what you think.

I need to see it.

I'm so turned on right now

Me too

I better go

I can't be at full mast around all these kids.

LOL! 

If it's not too weird, send me some pics of
Gymboree.... I want to see the mayhem

I will. But I now have in writing you
asked for pics

Yes, yes. Ok.

So cute!!

I want to go

Was it fun?

It was an experience. They played all the hits: Pizza. Cake. Gift bags of crap

Did you get me a gift bag?!

Did she have fun?

It was cute seeing her be the center of attention

Awwweeee!!!

Because I'm not a pedophile – I had no idea what Gymboree was

What the hell is it?

It's basically gymnastics for little kids

I had no idea!

Are you still coming over later?

Yes, I'll call you when I'm on my way

Can't wait!

FEELING TINGLY

Sun, May 25 at 10:32pm

My football team lost today

I'm so sorry to hear that

Do you even remember what my team is?

Tampa Bay, silly

You remembered!!!

Of course, I listen to everything you say

It's so weird that I love football and you love romantic comedies

I'm a sensitive man

Yes you are. But what does that make me?

A beautiful woman

Stop it

It's true. You're smart. Sophisticated. Funny. Caring.

I wish you were undressing me right now...

If I wasn't in Chicago I would be

Oh yeah? What would you do...

I would start by kissing every inch of your body...

Which part first?

Your neck...

Slowly moving down till you start to squirm...

What about my mouth?

Then I work my way back up to your neck and slowly kiss your lips...

Mmmmm...

I moan in your ear. You can feel how turned on I am....

More...

Then I kiss my way down your body and slowly remove your panties...

Very slowly...

Then I kiss your stomach and inner thighs.

Is that all?

Are you asking for more?

Begging!!!

I tease you for a while... kissing around your wetness

It literally makes the parts of my body you're talking about warm

Then I lick you gently

Very soft and slow

Pinching your nipples the entire time

I love that

You're moaning. You're really close.

So I slow down

Tease you

This is so hot

I want to do all that

Have you been touching yourself?

No, but I'm getting all hot and bothered

Feeling tingly

Yum

I keep thinking about grazing my fingers down your back

I just felt you doing that

All you have to do is say it

You're so fucking hot

Can't wait to have the real thing when you're back

Me too

I'm getting sleepy

Sweet dreams

Good night 😘

SPEED BUMP

Wed, May 26 at 8:12pm

I've tried to call you a few times, but no answer?

I know. I'm sorry

It's cool if you need space. I just wanted to make sure you know I'm here when you're ready to talk

I know. And thank you for saying that. I'm just trying to process everything

You're the most incredible woman I've ever met, we can work this out

Really?

Yes. Absolutely.

I'm sorry, I screamed at you at dinner

And they kicked us out

It's totally fine

But what if I want kids and you don't how can this ever work out?

I think in general it's really hard to find the right person.

But I think I've found the right person now.

So I have to believe that we can work this out.

No matter how difficult

Promise?

Promise.

I've been looking for you my whole life, I'm not going to blow it

Can you come over?

I need to see you

Yes. Give me an hour

To be clear, I just want to talk

Me too

Oh, ok, good

So don't even try to seduce me

Haha!

See you soon beautiful.

DELETING THE POSSIBILITIES

Fri, May 28 at 5:58pm

I'm at Costco you need anything? I hear they have good deals

Yes, I need throw pillows!!!!

Okay, let me look for some kirkland throw pillows in a 200 pack.

Wait, what in the world are you doing at Costco?

That seems like such a pedestrian activity for you

There's a few items here that they have a really good deal on lady

Haha! I can so hear you saying that!!!

Hey lady!

I'm sitting at a starbucks making lesson plans and laughing out loud. People are starting to stare

Ha!!

What do you buy there?

Mostly Claritin. It's so cheap here.

Please tell me you're not cooking meth

Is Claritin in meth?

Yes!

Wow. So cool

So you're a Costco member just to buy Claritin?

Oh, no. I'm not a member. I would never join a club.

But you have to be a member to buy stuff, right?

Yes.

Are you with someone?

No, I walk around for an hour. Eat free samples Then I befriend someone and convince them to let me stand in line with them Then I use their membership. And I pay them cash

And you don't think that's strange?

Now that I typed it and you're asking, yeah... I think it's weird.

This is your version of shower pissing!!!!

Haha!!!! YES!

I think we all piss in the metaphorical shower in our own special way

HAHA! These are things I do when I'm single. I do weird shit

Well, you're not single now.

I'm not?

No.

Are you saying you're my girlfriend?

Are you saying you're my boyfriend?

Yes

Yes

So we're exclusive?

Yes. Exclusive.

And that means deleting dating apps too

Yes. Doing it now

Me too

So it's official

Yes, it's official

I don't think I've ever liked someone as much as I like you

I feel the same 😍

I think we should celebrate our new title

Definitely!!!

Dinner tomorrow?

Sounds lovely

Who knew that going to Costco would land me a girlfriend.

LOL!

DON'T BE THAT WAY

Sun, May 30 at 6:16pm

I have to cancel dinner

What?

There's an emergency

Are you ok?

Yes

Ok... what's going on?

My sister's dog needs emergency surgery

Oh my god, was it hit by a car?

No. It has a herniated disk

Wow. What happened?

It fell down the stairs

Poor guy

I know

But it's your sister's dog, right?

So?

Can't she take it?

We were together when it happened

I hope the dog is ok, but you're really going to miss our dinner celebration cause of this?

I have to

You don't have to

She needs me

You'll never understand cause you're not a dog person

Yes, I couldn't possibly understand owning a dog. Thank you for clarifying

Come on, don't be that way

Seriously? Maybe you should reread the texts above and see "what way you're being"

I don't understand?

Do I have to spell it out for you?

I guess so

You're choosing a dog over me.

Not your dog. Your sister's dog.

You can't look at it that way

How else should I look at it?

That I'm trying to help someone

Wow, ok. Have fun.

We can reschedule our dinner, it's not a big deal

It's a big deal to me

I'm sorry

You honestly believe that you're making the right decision in this moment?

Yes, she needs me

We were supposed to be celebrating us?!

This is too much right now, I'll call you later.

Don't bother.

OH NO

Mon, May 31 at 1:49pm

I called you 5 times today...

Are you going to pick up?

WHO'S SECOND FIDDLE

Tue, Jun 1 at 3:12pm

Is this really the way you want to deal with this?

??

Seriously, you're not mature enough to answer the phone or text me back?

Tue, Jun 1 at 7:24pm

Since you're not calling me back I'm just going to type what I wanted to say...

I'm really sorry that you were upset. I know it was an important dinner for us

But you have to realize that my sister is very important to me. And when she needs my help I'm going to be there for her I'm doing the best I can

JUST TWO WORDS

Wed, Jun 2 at 4:39pm

I called my best friend Kendra in DC, so I could get some outside perspective...

I asked her what she thought and she sided with you. And she made me realize that if I want someone in my life, I have to choose them over my sister

You must know how much you mean to me

I love spending time with you and I only want more

I made a HUGE mistake and I'm sorry

Beautiful?

Yes my sweet!

Thank you for saying all that. I really appreciate it

Of course

I just needed you to apologize

Thank you

I mean it

I really missed you

I missed you too

I'm at work, can't really talk now

Can I come over after?

Yes. I can't wait to see you!

Me too

I'M FLATTERED

Thu, Jun 3 at 12:01pm

What does your day look like?

Besides looking ridiculously sexy?

Ha! I don't know about all that

I think you do

Stop it

You stop it

I'm trying to get work done

Then stop responding

I can't

Good

Oh! I forgot to ask you...

Yes

Will you be my date to the teacher of the year dinner?

I would be honored

Yay! It's a brunch with boring teachers and my principal just warning you

Will you be there?

What?! Of course!

Then it will be amazing

You're so sweet. I'm so glad you're coming!

Me too. I'm honored to be invited

I can't wait for you to meet all the people I work with

I can finally put faces with names

And tell Ms. Jenny what I really think of her

No. You can't say anything!!!

I'm just kidding. I would never say anything to her in front of you

Good

I would wait till you go to the bathroom.

No!!!

Ok, I'll restrain myself

Haha!

It will be fun!

A GOOD HEADLINE

Sat, Jun 5 at 1:06am

Oh boy, my neighbor is baaaack

What's he doing?

Texting me

Fun times

He wanted to know if his vacuuming was too loud

Is that a euphemism?

Haha! I don't think so?

It might be another go to pick up line.
I used to use that one a lot when I
was younger

LOL!!!

I asked him how he even knew I was home

What'd he say?

That my lights were on

Creepy because it's not like he has to
walk by your place to get to his

You're right, that is creepy

Yes it is. Want a pro tip?

Yes

Stop texting him

Haha! I think you're right!!

If he kills you in your sleep, I promise I'll show this text exchange to the police

Ok, now you're scaring me

No need to be afraid. Take solace in the fact that you know who your killer is, most don't ever find out

Stop it!! Seriously!

I would if I could. These are just facts

Great, now I'm really scared

Come on, don't be

I am

Dog walking vacuuming guy is not going to hurt you

Are you sure?

Now that I typed that, it does read like a good headline.

Stop it!!!!

You wouldn't even care if I died

If I didn't care why did I offer to send the text to the police? Hmmm? Your logic is very thin

Fine. But I'm still scared

If you're being serious, I could come over

It's 1am. I couldn't ask that of you

I would do anything for you

Really?

Of course. I would murder the neighbor if I had to.

Awwwwe

I'm on my way

Thank you

Just need to grab my vacuum and a leash

STOP IT!!

GET THE STICK OUT OF YOUR ASS

Mon, Jun 7 at 3:29pm

There's been something bothering me, but I don't know how to bring it up

What is it?

It's come up a few times...

You can say anything to me

The other night when I asked you to go to karaoke and you didn't want to go?

Yeah?

It's hard to say this because I don't want you getting mad

It's okay, just say it. I won't

You're not fun

Ok...?

You've got a lot of great qualities, but you're too ridged

You like to push everyone's buttons around you but you don't like yours pushed

So what are you saying?

I want you to be more spontaneous

How so?

Like you're only fun on your terms

You don't like to do things if they're not scheduled or your idea

137

I can see that

It's really important to me that you're more free

Ok

Sometimes I just want to drop everything and go out
of town

Or go dancing on a whim

And I'd like you to be there with me

That was hard to hear, but thanks for
saying all this

Are you open to it?

Of course

I want to do everything with you

Even if it means being less rigid?

Even if it means being less ridged

Promise

Promise

COLOR

Wed, Jun 9 at 5:55pm

I'm freaking out

What's wrong?

I'm getting my haircut and I think I've made a giant mistake with the color

I'm sure it's perfect

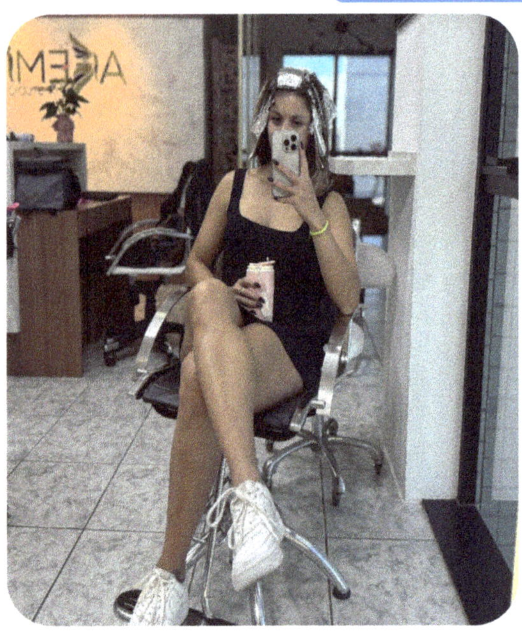

You look beautiful! I'm sure it's going to work b/c you can pull anything off

Liar

Come on

I look like I'm preparing for an alien invasion!! And the color is going to be terrible!

Stop it

I'm going to look like a train wreck for my birthday

I think you look perfect.

Really?

You're not just saying that?

Gorgeous.

Wed, Jun 9 at 6:43pm

I'm home now. I think I can live with it

What do you think?

See. Gorgeous

You're so hot

HAIRCUT DEBUT

Thu, Jun 10 at 7:31am

Happy Birthday!!!!!

Thank you! You're the first one to say so!

Please allow me to be the second...

HAPPY BIRTHDAY!!

Haha!! Thank you!

I'm so excited to meet your family

Me too!

I've been brushing up on all my racist small talk, so I feel ready

HAHA!

They're going to love you!

See you in a little bit

SIDE EFFECTS

Fri, Jun 11 at 9:11am

I love your dad

Well, he loves you!

They all loved you

Even your sister? I couldn't tell

Especially my sister

That's good to hear

How could they not you're so charming and lovely

Stop it.

You know you are

Your mom looks REALLY good for having had surgery

She's finally getting back to being herself

I didn't know her before the surgery, but she's really sweet and caring. She's nothing like you described

Well that's not who she was before. So you're getting the best version, trust me

I think chemo made her a better person

They should add that to the side effects list

LOL!!!!!

Oh, don't let me forget to give you your birthday present

What?! You got me a present?!!

Yes. You didn't think I forgot did you?

I wasn't sure. I thought you weren't into presents

I'm not, but I am for you

What is it?

I'm not telling…

Please

No

How about a hint?

Absolutely not

Fine

Do you like puppies?

Yes! Oh my god you got me a puppy?!!!

No. That's the worst present you can get someone

But they're so cute

Yes, but it's like here's a gift that you can't return because you'll look like an asshole if you do, and if you keep it it's a 15 year commitment

But they're so cute

I want to start a business called Rent-a-puppy so you can always have the best part of the experience

But what happens to them when they get older?

We don't ever talk about that part of the business model. Ever.

That's so sad

I'm going to give it to you tomorrow

I can't wait!

Woof woof!!

I DON'T KNOW HOW TO HANDLE YOU

Sun, Jun 13 at 2:50pm

What are you up to?

LOVE it!! So frickin' cute!!!!!

I'm a damn good babysitter if I do say so myself

You know how to get me with those cute Penelope pics

I thought it was pretty high on the cuteness scale

You're playing dirty by sending me those. You and a cute little kid

Sorry, that was not my intention

You asked, and that was the answer

I know

I want more

Are you sure?

Yes.

It's just playing dirty

This isn't some high level psychological test, I'm just sharing pics of me babysitting my niece. That's it.

I know, but you know it's what I want

Then I'm not going to send more, this is crazy

Send them

You're like a junkie

I know, it just melts my heart

I sincerely don't know what to do

More please

Last one…

OMG!!! Stop it. Right now

I was trying to

I can't handle it

New rule. No more pictures

That's not fair

I think it's for the good of the whole.
I'm sorry I sent it in the first place

Don't be

It's just hard because you know it's what I want and
you don't

I know. I'm sorry

THE TALK

Tue, Jun 15 at 7:06pm

I think we need to talk

Ok...

It's nothing bad

Now I know it's really bad

I promise, it's not

Ok. Then just say it now

It's not really a text conversation

Okay

Tomorrow?

Sure

I'll come to yours

BUT MAYBE
WE CAN

I know we agreed not to talk for a week, but I really miss you

I'm not gonna lie, it's been really hard

I really want to see you

Me too

What are you doing?

I'm at my parent's friends lake house

Nice. I'm jealous

Are you alone?

No. it's that girls weekend I told you about.

It's my sister and several girlfriends

Oh, cool

I look at your pictures everyday

You do?

Yes. Why is this so hard?

Because we're meant to be together and can work this out

Really?

YES. Do you not think so?

Not sure

Well, I'm sure

You are?

Zero doubt.

I love that about you

What?

Your confidence

I miss you

I like hearing that

I really like you

I really like you too

When did you know you first liked me?

I knew the day I met you

Me too, but I mean when was the moment that you felt more?

It was the day we met

I was so down and depressed. My friends were taking me out for a drink to try and cheer me up

But no one. I mean no one. Can get me out of that place. Not my sister Not Kendra

Sometimes it lasts for weeks

But then you came over to the table and made me laugh instantly

And then kept making me laugh. I knew

I had no idea

What about you?

For me it happened on our first date.

When you complimented that woman's dress and then she secretly paid for our dinner

When people meet you they want to do things for you. Help you. Give to you

You have this ability to open people up. Strangers up

And it's the most attractive thing in the world to me.

You just made me cry

I'm sorry, I should get back to my friends

Ok beautiful

THOSE GREEN EYES

Sun, Jun 20 at 10:23am

I'm so sorry I drunk dialed you last night

I'm glad you did

You are?

I just wish my ringer was on

I'm mortified

What were you going to say?

I don't know

Come on. You do

I want to try and make this work

Me too.

We need to try everything we can, so we know we tried

I agree

When are you back in town?

Tomorrow

Come over then

I'd like that

Can't wait to have you in my arms

I missed you a lot yesterday

What did you miss?

The twinkle in your eye/smile

Your voice

Your hug

Your beautiful green eyes when you first turn over and open them in the morning. Then you smile at me and say good morning

You just put a huge smile on my face

You always put a huge smile on my face

Admission:

I did look at the picture of you and Penelope for a while last night 😬

Admission:

I looked at all the pictures I have of you last night and everyday since I last saw you

Which one is your favorite?

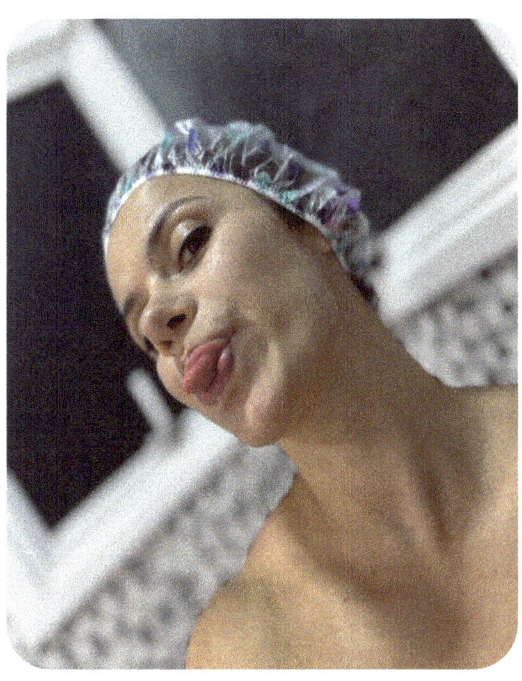

What?

Of all the pics you have of me, why that one?

It makes me laugh every time. I love it

That's sweet

Can't wait to see you

Me too

IT'S OFFICIAL

Tue, Jun 22 at 9:17am

I love you.

I love you too 

Feels so scary/good to type it for the first time

I've never said it to anyone before

I'm so glad it's to me and not your neighbor

Hey! Leave him out of this

I was going to ask if you've said it before, but I know the answer

Doesn't matter the answer, because you're the one for me

I love you so much

I love you more

SISTER LOGIC

Thu, Jun 24 at 3:36pm

I'm so annoyed 😤 😤

What happened beautiful?

I loaned my sister my car and she scratched it

That sucks.

But like a big scratch

The whole right side.

And it's dented!

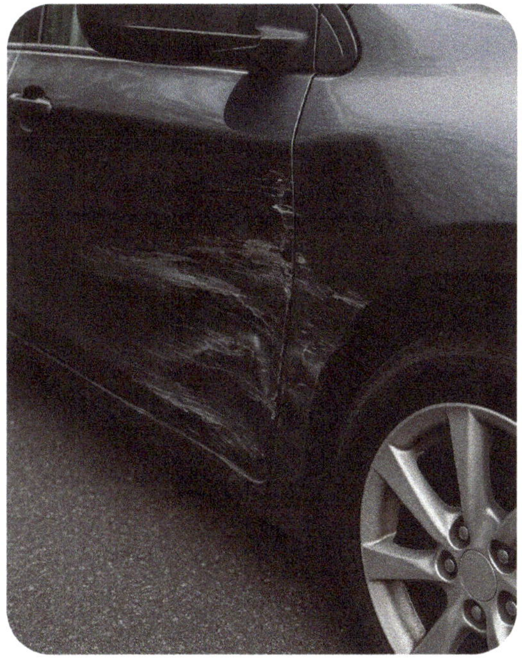

Jesus, that's not good.

The worst part is she didn't even tell me she did it

What?!

Yeah, she returned the car and didn't even mention it

That's really fucked up

I know. I only noticed it when I got in the car to go to work

Did you confront her about it?

No.

But you are going to, right?

I don't think so

What?!!! Why?

She can't afford to fix it, and I know she didn't do it on purpose

If someone borrows your car, it's their responsibility to return it in the same if not better condition.

Maybe

Not maybe? They absolutely should

This is an opportunity to set better boundaries with her

What are you talking about?

You're not 8 anymore, you don't have to share everything with her

You just don't understand

I do understand. I think you don't

I'm not having this conversation with you

If you replace your sister's name with another name in this same exact scenario how would you be reacting?

I'd be pissed. Which I am!

Right. But then what would you do about it?

I'd ask them to get it fixed.

Right. The same logic applies here too

I don't need you telling me how to have a conversation with my sister

Well someone has to b/c it's not healthy

This is what we talked about the other night

No, it's not.

Yes, it is.

You want me to be more open minded about having kids and I need you to make room for me in your life

I have been

I agree you have been. But this is a new example of where I'm asking to be let in

I don't like it

I'm sure you don't. But you need to call her and demand she pay for the damage.

I'm not comfortable with that

If you want me to be open to all the things you want, you have to be open to what I want too

Fine.

I'll think about it

Thank you

TEARS

Fri, Jun 25 at 6:45pm

I spoke to my sister about the car

Really?

Yes

And?

I told her how pissed I was and that she needed to pay

That's amazing

She said she won't pay and explained that it was some how my fault because the backside window was dirty and she couldn't see the pole that she hit.

Ok... and what did you say?

My instincts were to agree with her

Ok, well it's a big step that you even confronted her.

BUT then I told her that that was bullshit and she needed to pay

Ok, wow

Then she burst into tears

Sucks that she cried, but good for you for standing up for yourself

She cries to get her way, that's her thing

Either way, that's an amazing first step

I didn't want to do it, but now that I did I feel
MUCH better

Thank you for pushing me

I love you 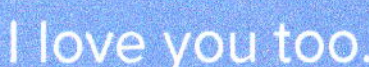

I love you too.

YOU HEARD ME

Sat, Jun 26 at 3:22pm

What are you doing tonight?

No plans...

Good.

You're wearing this....

I'm wearing this...

What?!

Amazon is delivering them to my house in 2 hours

I'm so excited! 😁 😁 😁

Where are we doing?

We're going to the magic castle!

I've never been!

I know

Then after we're going back to this spot....

I'm so turned on right now

Come over now.

Ok! Leaving now

WORK AND PLAY

Tue, Jun 29 at 1:00pm

What would you be doing to me right now if we were having sex?

Where are you?

Thinking about taking care of business on my balcony...

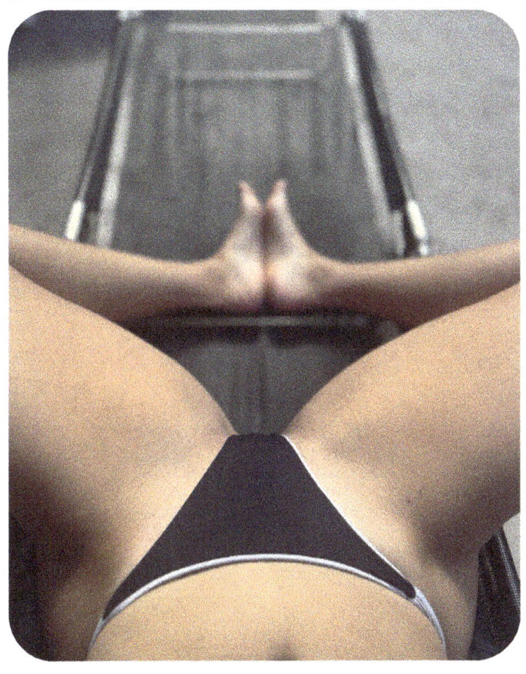

Where are you?

In a sales meeting

I'm so sorry

I'll leave you alone, but I still want you to come over tonight

You do huh?

Actually, I demand it.

Well, maybe we should try something new

What'd you have in mind?

Well, it would involve a lot trust b/c it's something you said you don't do…

I never said there's something I wouldn't do

Yes you did

Oh, that!!

Yes.

You do like to play down there a lot…

Yes, I do

Mmmmm, let me think about it

Seriously, no pressure.

BOUNDARIES

Sun, July 4 at 11:43am

Where are you?

I haven't left yet

What?!

Everything took longer than I thought

And you're just telling me now?!

Sorry

You know how I feel about being late. WTF?

I know. I know. Sorry.

Sorry's not good enough

I'm leaving now

You're already 15 mins late, so when do you plan on getting here?

Waze says 40 mins

Seriously, don't bother

I'm coming. I want to meet Rebecca

If you wanted to meet Rebecca, you would have been here on time

I thought it was a party. What's the big deal?

If you don't know, then that's on you.

THE PUSH BACK

Wed July 7 at 10:39pm

When am I going to see you next?

You know how busy my week is

I know, I was just being playful

Sorry, just stressed and I'm on my period

Maybe we could go to the movies on Sunday?

You know I have book club

But what about after?

Let's just play it by ear.

Do you not want to see me?

Of course I do. It's just tricky right now

I really want to see you

Let's just talk later

WAY BACK

Fri, July 9 at 2:13pm

Do you want me to come over later?

I do, but I told Jenny I'd help her with her closet

Ok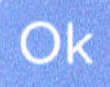

I'll call you later

Let's talk tomorrow, I'm gonna call Jack and hit Malone's

INSECURITIES

Sun, July 11 at 4:27pm

I didn't like our conversation earlier

I'm tired of you being weird with me for wanting to see you.

Like I said, I really love you and do want to see you

But I've been neglecting my friends and I need to make them a priority too

I get it. I love that you have so many friends...

But we went from being inseparable to barely seeing each other really quickly

Is something else going on?

No. I'm just trying to find a balance.

Your over correction has been difficult to deal with

It makes me feel like you don't want to be with me

You know I want to be with you. I've made that very clear

Are you seeing someone else?

What?! No.

I just need to have my own life too

But aren't I apart of your life?

Isn't the point of being with someone to see if you want to and can spend the rest of your life with that person?

I guess

I haven't seen you all week

You need to give me, us, more time than this

I see what you're saying

And I'm not saying you shouldn't hang out with your friends

We just need to find the right balance with us

I hear you

Thank you

Can I come over tonight?

I'd love that

THERE FOR YOU

Tue, July 13 at 2:44pm

You there?

I am now

I tried to call

Sorry, I'm at work. About to go into another meeting

Sorry. We can talk later

What's going on? Are you ok?

My childhood friend, Cindy, died 😭 😭

I'm so sorry beautiful. That's terrible news

She was the one with the lisp that lived across the street, right?

Yes

Where are you?

Driving home from the gym

First, please stop texting and driving

Can you come over?

Yes, but I won't be done for a while

Ok. What time?

8pm.

That's so late, but ok

Come over right after please

I will, I promise.

Are you coming?

Yes

But it's almost 8:30?!

I know my boss pulled me into a meeting and I left my phone was in my office.

I'm so sorry

It's ok. Maybe we should just talk tomorrow

What? No. I'm coming over

I think I just need to be alone

Are you sure?

I was going to bring that matzo ball soup you love and your favorite sparkling water.

And I was going to massage your feet while we watched 30 for 30

You were?

Yes. I'm just a little behind schedule. But I'm leaving now

Ok

See you soon

Thank you

Love you so much. 😍😍😍

YOU WANT ME TO COME

Thu, July 15 at 12:54pm

We can talk about this when I see you, but I wanted to plant the seed...

Excited. Ok. What is it?

My family is going to France in October for the grape harvest

Cool!

Our family friend has a villa there and we're all going to stay for a couple of weeks

That sounds incredible

I've been before, it's SO NICE!

And I want you to come

Really?! I'd love to!

YAY! Let's talk more when I see you later

Sounds great, I'll buy some champagne!

Love you!

Love you too

I'M SURE I TOLD YOU

Sun, July 18 at 2:22pm

How was the service?

Beautiful

But I learned that Cindy didn't die, she overdosed

Holy shit!

I know

That's fucking terrible

I know

How did you find that out?

Her brother told me

Wow

The family didn't want anyone to know

And he told you?

We used to be close

I told you, he was my first boyfriend in high school

Oh wow. I did not know that

I thought I told you?

I would've remembered that

Sorry, I thought I did

Ok

There's nothing to worry about we're just friends

It's a little weird you didn't tell me

You don't trust me?

Of course I trust you

Good.

It's just you're in another state, at a funeral with your ex boyfriend

Right, but it's not like that.

It's fine

Clearly it's not

I just think it's weird you didn't tell me

I haven't seen him in 10 years

Can you talk?

Can't. I'm going over to the family's house for the memorial now. We are in the car together

I know you have a weird thing with being friends with exs but nothing is going on here

Call me later

Love you.

Love you too

Sun, July 18 at 9:36pm

Zoey?

I tried to call but no answer. I'll be up

MESSY

Mon, July 19 at 8:21am

Hey! So sorry, my phone died last night

I didn't get your text till I got back to hotel

I've called you seven times this morning. Call me back.

Hello?

Mon, July 19 at 10:52am

I'm at work now can't talk

Call me later

Ok

Love you 😚 😚 😚

Mon, July 19 at 8:05pm

It's late here with the time change. I'm getting sleepy but really wanted to talk

What time will you be home?

I'm stuck at work with my boss. Can't talk

Let's just talk tomorrow when you're back

I'm sad we're not going to talk

I can call when I'm out, but I think you'll be asleep

Talk tomorrow

Sweet dreams

WE ALREADY TALKED ABOUT THIS

Wed, July 21 at 6:25pm

Sorry, I know we talked about this, but it's still driving me crazy that you think you can't be friends with exs??

It doesn't work

Even if you don't believe it, it's entirely possible to have someone in your life that you used to be intimate with

Of course it's possible, but is it healthy?

It's definitely healthy to have good people in your life.

People you care about

As I said before it's a question of whether you want your past in your present

It's a natural part of life. Life is messy

It's only a part of life if you make it part of life

Well, I'm ok having it as part of my life

I don't want it for me and if I'm being honest I don't really want it for you

Well, it's my decision

I know.

I thought you weren't the jealous type?

I'm not. I just don't want to be friends with your exs

No one's asking you to. You don't have to hang out
with them

I definitely won't be hanging out with
them, but thanks for the permission

I'm just saying that I want to be able to spend time
with them

Then you're saying that you're not
willing to let go of your past

Not at all!!!

We shared an important time, and I don't want them
out of my life forever

If you don't see the flaws in that way
of thinking, then you should do it

Ugh. You're the worst

Thank you.

This is so frustrating

Agreed

Fine. Then I won't meet him for coffee

I only want you to do what you want
to do

Don't do it for me

I know
For the record, I think you're being too uptight

I strongly disagree. This is about how you want to live your life.

It's VERY different

And don't tell me I'm uptight because I don't want to play with your exs or mine

Fine.

Fine.

WITHHOLDING

Fri, July 23 at 3:59pm

I just ran into Jack at Trader Joes

He's the best

Is there something you want to tell me?

I don't think so

What were you doing while I was at the funeral?

What are you talking about?

You went to the FUCKING swingers party with Jack?!! That's what!!!

Can I call you?

No.

Did you go?

Well?????

I did

What the fuck!!!!! 😡

Clearly you not cool with that. Now I know

I don't give a fuck about swingers parties, as long as nothing happened

What I do give a fuck about is you not TELLING ME YOU WENT TO ONE!!!!

Yeah, while you were at a funeral with your ex-boyfriend that you didn't tell me about

I told you nothing happened!!!

So what? You went to get back at me?!!

How old are you?

We said we'd always be honest with each other

I know

You failed!

You're right

I fucked up

I'm so pissed

I know

I need some space.

SMOOTH IT OVER

Mon, July 26 at 4:08pm

So, I got 4 tickets to Wicked...

What?!!!

Yep

You're not joking right? I don't think I could handle it because I'm still kinda pissed at you.

I wouldn't do that to you

I'm freaking out!!!

Ha!

How did you get them? There are impossible to get

You never mind how I got them

Who else are we taking?

I thought we'd invite your parents

Awwwww, that's so sweet

Your mom mentioned wanting to see it, so I thought they'd like it

They absolutely will!!!

You want to ask them?

YES. Texting them now

WALMART

Thu, July 29 at 2:11pm

It finally happened...

What?

Dog walking neighbor asked me out

He finally worked up the courage.

I'm proud of him

He was so nervous before he asked he tripped over his dog leash and scrapped his leg.

Oh my gosh

I felt so bad for him

It was really hard not to laugh in his face

How'd he do it

He asked me if I wanted to go to Walmart with him

What did you tell him?

I went on a rant about how terrible Walmart is for the world and the environment

And then?

He was even more embarrassed that he asked

Just for the record, I don't think he was asking you out.

What?!

I think he was asking you to go to Walmart

No way. He was asking me out

Ahhhhh, no

Shut up.

He did

You mentioned he doesn't have a car, right?

Yes, he rides his bike everywhere

Don't you think that maybe he just needed a ride to Walmart?

I hate you right now

I'm just saying

He was legit asking me out. I can tell the difference

Ok. Then what did you say?

I said no!!!

Poor guy, how's he going to get that new bookshelf he's been wanting and that rice cooker?

It was a date!!!

You're very attractive, so I can see why you'd think that.

I'm going to tell him I'm going to go with him

So you'd be going on a date while we're in an exclusive relationship?

Wouldn't that be cheating?

I hate you right now

This is how I feel right now!

Please tell me you weren't texting and driving this entire time?

I'm in traffic light!

There's something seriously wrong with you

Call me later so you don't kill yourself

Please don't respond

TEARS OF JOY

Sat, July 31 at 3:10pm

So I'm at the mall...

And...

And you know how I'm obsessed with girls butts in jeans.

Yes. It's one of many very strange hobbies you have

But I think the universe has finally heard me

What are you talking about?

At Bloomingdales they have a machine.

And the machine scans your body.

That's not a sentence I ever thought I'd read.

It looks like that scary new metal detector at the airport.

The one where you raise your hands over your head and don't move.

Yes!

Here....

The machine scans your body and then it prints out a list of all the brands of jeans in the exact size that's the right fit for you body

Wow!!

It tells you the exact correct size in all the brands they carry. It's nuts.

This is how you're spending your day? 

I've been here for hours. Watching women try on and then buy the correct jeans

That sounds creepy

No it's beautiful. I cried when I saw it

You cried?

Teared up

Do you need me to come get you?

No, I'm good. I think I might try and get a part time job here.

You have a full time job.

I know, but I think it would be so satisfying.

For Christmas I'm getting you a gift certificate to a psychiatrist

THE PINK ONES

Mon, August 2 at 12:40pm

Are you in a sales meeting already?

Unfortunately, yes

There's just something about this time of day

I'm dripping, thinking about you...

Oh yeah?

What are you going to do about it?

After work, I'm coming to your place

I want you showered

Freshly shaven

In bed

Naked

Except for pink panties with the lace that I got you, and the black high heels

Done

I want to try that thing we talked about

Really?

I love the idea of how naughty it is...

I'm so turned on right now

Good.

See you soon...

GETTING SWEATY

Fri, August 6 at 3:19pm

My parents wanted me to tell you thank you again for wicked. They loved it!!

Oh good! I'm so glad!

My dad apologized profusely again about falling asleep

Ha! Best $400 nap of his life.

I was mortified. I'm so sorry

It's not your fault

I know. It's just embarrassing

It's fine

Well it was fine till he started snoring

Stop it. I'm getting sweaty, it's making me so uncomfortable

We were only in the second row, I'm sure the cast didn't notice

LOL!!!! Stop it. Oh my god, it's so terrible. 😬 😬

Seriously, it's fine.

I understand if you don't want to go to France anymore

I wouldn't miss it for anything

Really?

Yes. I love you and your family. Every weird, racist snoring inch.

Where did I find you?

In a bar. Did you forget? Jenga?

Haha! No, I mean how did I get so lucky?

Believe me, I'm the lucky one

GET A CLUE

Sat, August 29 at 6:47am

Happy Birthday!!!!

Thank you beautiful!!

You're up early

Member how I told you I was planning something?

Yes

Are we finally watching Harry Met Sally?

No...

If I'm meeting Meg Ryan And Billy Crystal I don't think I can handle that!!

I'll literally explode

No!

You're going to put on your Billy Crystal sweater from the movie and your ill fitting jeans and I'll be dressed like Meg Ryan from the orgasm scene

Then we are going all around the city (even though I know this isn't New York) and will be recreating all of your favorite scenes from the movie.

I have friends and actors waiting all over town!

Shut the fuck up!

Really?!

I'm waiting out front.

I definitely going to explode

Hurry!

I'm coming!

LIKE I PROMISED

Mon, August 31 at 10:14am

It's been two days but I'm still hungover

But that was the BEST. MOST AMAZING BIRTHDAY I've ever had

Really?

Oh god. YES. THANK YOU

I can't imagine how much work that was.

I'm blown away

I love you

I love you more

Here's your last present...

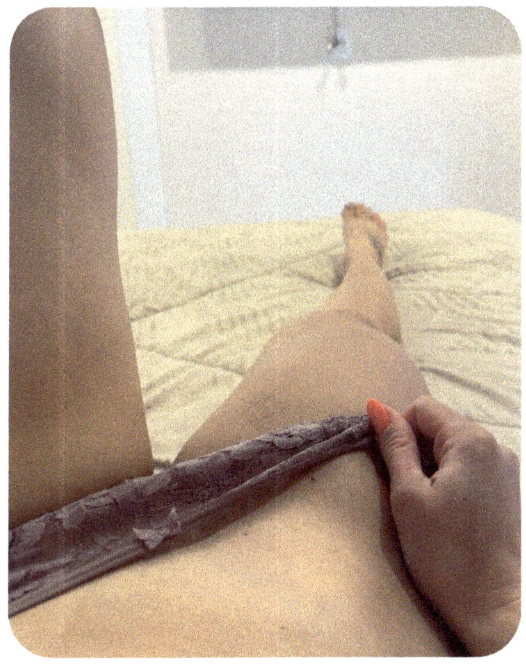

Sweet Jesus!

ROW Z

Tue, September 8 at 1:30pm

Remember how my sister booked all the tickets to France?

Yes

Well, she booked my seat next to hers

Ok

And you're in the back of the plane

So I'm no where near you?

Sitting alone?

Yes

Can't we just switch the seats?

I called the airline, they can't move you because the flight is full.

That sucks. It's like an 11 hour flight

We could try at the gate to get you moved

Or you moved?

I thought we could all sit together

Sure, but if it comes down to it I want to sit with you

Right

So maybe we can ask if your sister can switch with me?

Hello?

Maybe. She did book them though

What does that mean?

Nothing

We still paid for the tickets!

I know what you're saying

It doesn't sound like you do

That you want to sit together

Right and...

And that's it

That's not just it. Do you want to sit with me?

Of course. But if we can't it's not the end of the world

It's that you're choosing her over me, again

No, I'm not

Ok. I don't have the energy for this right now

This doesn't have to be a thing. We can work it out at the airport

It's not about the fucking seat!

Come on

Let's just talk later

PLEASE HEAR ME

Tue, September 15 at 9:15pm

Hello?

Are you really not going to go to France?

Come on

Don't you think you're being a little dramatic?

I know you think I'm being ridiculous

But it matters

I hear you, but loosen the fuck up

It will still be fun even if we don't sit next to each other

I get that, but this keeps coming up. Over and over

I know you don't think much of it, but to me it's a big deal and a huge indicator as to whether or not we can build a life together.

If we ever did have a kid where would I rank in the pecking order? The kid, your sister, then your needs, then me?

I understand

But do you agree?

Yes

I don't want to. But yes

I want you to do whatever you want, it's just important to me that I'm heard

You're annoying

But I hear you

That's all I'm asking

And BTW, I'm still going to France silly

I'm not that crazy

Can I come over tonight?

Yes. I'd love that

YOU HEARD

Fri, September 18 at 10:11am

Guess what?

I love you

I love you too, but that's not it

What?

My sister agreed to switch seats!

Amazing!

Yay! I'm so excited!!!

Me too

See, I do listen

You're so fucking hot right now

Me...?

Yes, you

I don't know about all that

Let's go to karaoke tonight.

But don't you have your poker game tonight?

Not anymore

Seriously?!

Yes.

Yay!!! Fun! Let's do it

I just want to mentally prepare you, I'm a terrible singer

Don't worry, I got you!

JUST WHEN I THOUGHT I KNEW YOU

Thu, October 1 at 10:46pm

I'm soooooo excited for our trip!

Me too!

I'm still need to pack

I'm the worst at packing I never know how to get it all in

You can put some in mine if you need to, I'm not bringing that much stuff.

This is where I'm at....

Oh my gosh!!! I can't stop laughing

It's not funny! It's a condition 😐 🤓

Why are you bringing a snorkel and fins?

They have a pool. You know I can't hold my breath

But it's going to be freezing

I'll have you know the pool is heated

I don't know what to say other then this just makes one more thing about you that I adore

Thank you

I love you so much

I love you more 😘

SOUR GRAPES

Those were some of my favorites

You really captured some magical moments in such vivid clarity! LOL!!

That was a magical trip. Thank you so much for inviting me!!! I didn't think it was possible but I've fallen more in love with you

TOO MUCH

Thu, October 22 at 7:58pm

Hello?

I called you earlier, you didn't call me back?

I know, crazy day at work. Parent/teacher conferences. Sorry

Will I see you later?

I'm still jet lagged. I just want to go home and sleep

Ok

MISS YOU

Sat, October 24 at 10:10am

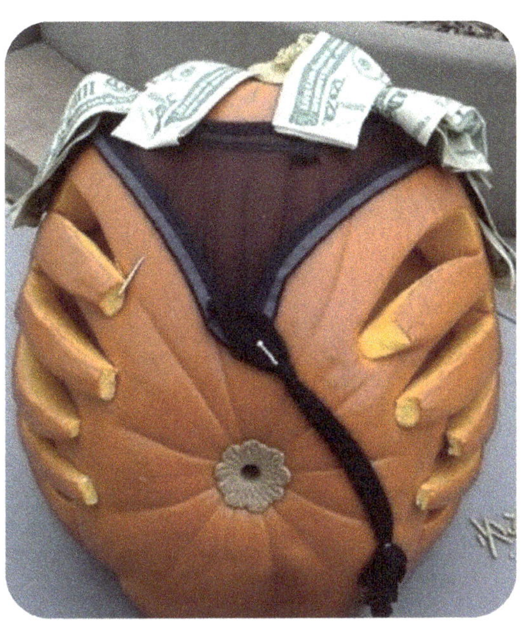

Oh my god, that is very disturbing!

It's stripper pumpkin

Please tell me you didn't make that?!

I wish

Sad I won't see you tonight

Me too

I really wanted to spend our first Halloween together

You sure you can't come?

I told you, I'm spending time with Jennifer

I know

I was just trying to be cute

Have fun

OH NO

Wed, October 28 at 1:11pm

Can you meet tonight?

Yes. Should I come to your house?

Let's meet at Casa

You want to meet out?

Yes

I'm kinda tired

Let's get a drink.

You sure?

Yes

Ok

SHE DID IT

Fri, October 30 at 11:01pm

It seems impossible to think of my life without you

I love you more than you'll ever know

I so wish we wanted the same happy ending

You are such an amazing person

Not being together is the most difficult thing I have ever had to do

It makes me so sad 😭 😭

I know. Me too

DEVASTATED

Wed, November 4 at 9:29pm

Since you won't answer my calls...

I need to tell you that I feel like I'm being punished for being completely honest with you and it doesn't sit well with me

You're not being punished

But I am

It's just not true

Then why'd you break up with me?

It's not that simple

Any other guy would've lied to you. I told you the truth

Any other guy, really?

Yes

Any guy would've strung you along and pretend they wanted kids.

They would've taken it as far as they could for as long as they could and then you would've found out the truth

I would never do that to you

But by being straight up with you and completely honest with you — you break up with me?!

Come on, it's just not this black and white

Your solution is to break up with me!

You made it that black and white!

A normal person would want to try and work it out.

We did try

I can't keep getting closer to you and falling deeper and deeper in love if our goals don't line up.

Can't we date for at least a year and make sure we are even right for each other before we have a serious conversation about kids?!

I can't do this over text. Calling you now...

THE UNDOING

Sat, November 7 at 2:09pm

I don't want to go to this wedding without you

I really wish I was going with you

Everyone is going to be asking about you, and I'm not ready to talk about it

I'm having a really really hard time with you not in my life

It's really hard and painful for me to think of you there without me

I miss you so much

I don't know what to say

Sat, November 7 at 11:26pm

I am leaving the venue now and it's so hard for me not to go over to your place...

When does this get better?

Nights are so hard without you

JUMBLED UP

Sun, November 8 at 9:43am

I didn't text you back because I don't know what to say...

I'm just so angry

I feel broken. Crushed.

I'm not mad. I understand

THE EXCHANGE

Wed, November 18 at 11:45am

Here are the final charges on my credit card...

The rental car was $624.54. Looking at my statement the quote they gave us was in Euros. So it's more than we thought.

That dinner was $483.11

$624.54 plus $483.11 divided by 2 = $553.83

I guess just subtract that total from what I owe you from the hotels and venmo the rest

Sending this text feels so final. I didn't want to send it.

But after I saw the pillows at my door...

You can pick the date/time/place, but I want to meet and give you your things

Do you want to meet this afternoon?

I have a meeting on main st but it should be over around 2pm

I could come over to your place. Let me know if that sounds good

I have a meeting at 2. Can u come here before?

I can come over now. Does that work?

Yes. Can you give me 20 mins?

Sure, no problem. I will be there in 30.

SINCE MIDDLE SCHOOL

Thu, November 19 at 11:57am

Thank you for our talk yesterday

I really want to figure this out

It would be so nice if we got a happy ending

I hope you don't want this to end with a hand job. Because that'd be weird.

There's the ridiculous man I love!!!

But seriously, are you turning down a hand job?

I haven't turn one down since my first one in middle school, thank you very much

Do you want to meet up and continue our conversation?

What about saturday afternoon?

That works

Good. I'll bring the lotion

ONE LAST TIME

Sat, November 21 at 10:08pm

I wanted to kiss you really bad today...

I know. I did too. I wish I was over there now

Come over

I want to really badly

I want you to

Sleeping with you last time was incredible but the next day it made me feel so hollow and sad

I couldn't call you up and have you in my life.

I want you inside of me so badly but am scared that it's going to break my heart even more

I understand

I can't make this about sex right now

It's so much more

If this could be figured out through sex I would have you inside me for a week

Can't sex just be about sex sometimes?

I can't make it just about sex this time. I'm sorry.

I understand

Do you think we will get a happily ever after with our story?

I honestly don't know. But it's killing me

What do u think?

Being without you makes me so sad. This is a really hard place to be

Seems crazy we aren't together. I want to make it all better so badly

I do too

I keep searching for the perfect answer but can't find it.

YOU'RE GONNA GET IT

Fri, November 27 at 8:12pm

That helicopter is flying around my apartment...

Oh no, they're looking for you again

I hope they find me soon

They will. But when they do you're in big trouble.

Yes please to big trouble.

Huge trouble?

Picture the most trouble you've ever been in and triple it

I love your big trouble. I want big trouble now...

Call me later if u want to receive your punishment.

No. I want it now...

You can come get it if u want. I'm just warning you, you might be sore after

Are you home?

Yes

I was about to hop in the shower. But I'm home for the night

Do you want a visitor?

You better be wet by the time u knock on my door.

I'm dripping just thinking about seeing you.

Be there in 20 😘 😘

LINE IN THE SAND

Sat, November 28 at 11:15am

Last night was so hot

So hot

And you were right, I'm sore

I want you again, now...

Sat, November 28 at 7:20pm

Come on, don't you want to play with me

Of course I do

But like I said last night I can't keep doing that.

That's why I left

Can't we just play a little?

No. I need it all. Your touch and our post sex snuggles... our talks.

We have to stop this

I'm realizing that we have to be on the same page completely or it just won't work for me

Ok

THE LOOP

Mon, November 30 at 5:07pm

Can we talk?

I leave for DC tomorrow. Should we talk before I leave or when I return?

Tonight?

Going to the movies now, call you when I get home?

Mon, November 30 at 10:18pm

Actually, can we talk tomorrow? I'm battling some cramps

Yes. Call me in the morning or when you're feeling up to it

BREAKING THE RULES

Wed, December 2 at 5:55pm

I know we said no texting but I'm walking in a
blizzard in DC.

It's so beautiful and it makes me wish you were here

When does this get easier?

I wish we had a compromise to work
with

I wish you were here with me more than anything in
the world

Then be with me till you want a baby
and then break up with me

You'll be sick of me by then anyway

Can't you just have one baby with me?

Today that's all I could think about while hanging
with Kendra's newborn.

We would have so much fun together on that adventure

Her baby does the Penelope sucking thing.

Made me laugh but then I get sad because I couldn't tell you

Although I am breaking the break up rules and telling you now

I know. But imagine how much we can do without one.

Be with me.

Be with me till you can't be with me

We still have so much to do together. It could last a lifetime

But then I miss out on a baby

I could get swept up with you forever

Can't we just add a baby to our adventures?

We would be so awesome at it. It could be so much fun

I know we would. But if you chose not to have a baby I will expose you to a life you never thought was possible

I just need your love and a baby in a two years.

You have my love. Lots of it. We're so much more than just a baby

We could still do so much and have a baby though

If we did have a baby then you get everything you wanted and what am I left with?

I promise you a life of excitement, travel, laughter, amazing sex and so much more

Come on, that sounds pretty awesome

But we already have/had all that

If you get the baby. Something you want really bad. What're you going to promise me that's that big?

You get to be with the woman you love. Isn't that the dream?

But I'd say the same to you. Aren't I the dream?

Just to be with the man you love?

What would you like me to promise you?

I will give it

Hmmm. I'd have to think about it

I'm sorry to cut this off, but I'm heading to dinner now and I'm late

Do you want to talk after?

Will you be around or is it this a bad idea?

I can talk

Just so you know, your love is enough but one day I will want to add to that

Call you after

GOO-GOO-GA-GA

Thu, December 3 at 11:52am

I know I was really hard on you last night and I'm sorry.

That was an intense conversation

I was/am really hurting and don't know how to deal with all my feelings

And I'm sorry too. I'm in total baby mode here

I love you very much

I get back Sunday

Should we talk then?

Yes

And think more about what I can promise you

I have been, but no answer yet

And you think about what you'd like to promise me

I'd be promising you a baby. Have you not been keeping up with the conversation?!

Sorry. You're right

Let's just talk when I'm back

LET'S BE PARENTS

Sat, December 5 at 8:34pm

You'd make such a good dad

I know

Then why not?

Just because I'd make a good dad doesn't mean I should be a father

Yes it does

There's so many shitty parents out there, you'd be amazing

Just cause you'd be good at something doesn't mean you should do it. I'd make a great soldier too, but doesn't mean I want to go to war.

You're impossible

Life comes down to time. And kids take up a lot of time

I want that time for me and the things I can contribute to the world

That's selfish

No, having a kid is selfish

No, it's not

Yes, it is

It's the ultimate expression of love.

Bullshit. It's the most selfish act possible.

How?!

To have a half version of yourself running around that you can pump all your personal problems into? That's selfish.

You're so cynical

Maybe, but it's true

For you

For everyone!

It's like people who have cats and dogs. Ever wonder why all their pets end up with cancer?

Spoiler alert: because the animals are absorbing all their unresolved baggage and it's literally killing them

I don't want to do that to a kid

I'd rather spend that time on becoming a better person

Maybe we should talk later

Agreed.

THIS REALLY SHOULD BE A PHONE CALL

Sun, December 7 at 2:40am

Since our conversations seem to go round and round on the phone I wanted to put my thoughts in writing.

This is a collection of all the thoughts that keep going around in my head. I needed to get it out and I wanted you to see it as is without any back and forth...

I've been thinking a lot about our conversations over the past weeks and I had several epiphanies.

When I originally asked you if you wanted kids now, you said no. Right there we are on the same page. And when you asked me if I wanted kids ever, I said I could never say never, but I don't think I do.

And when I asked you if it was possible that you didn't want kids you said you'd have to leave that possibility open. We're still on the same page.

Then when we returned from France you turned it into an ultimatum. It was: commit to having kids right now (meaning at some point in the future) or it's over.

I could never make a clear choice with my back to the wall like that. To be totally frank, I gave you the most honest answer possible (I don't think I do, but I can never say never - and I must tell you that is most men's position on the subject).

But when it was put in such a way there was only one answer you'd accept and that's "yes I promise I want one" I couldn't be open to it.

But you are way to smart to know that if I "promised", I'd have the right to change my mind later (as would you).

So it's arbitrary because it's not dealing with the now... it's some idea of the future which may never come.

We could break up before then!

In regards to therapy. From my point of view you wanted me to go so I would change my mind. Which I would have been open to if you told me straight up that you'd be willing to change your mind too. Since you never would agree to that I don't want to go. For me to go, it had to be totally open on both sides. It's not.

In most of this time apart a lot of what's been said and asked feels like it was all about me changing my mind.

But what about you? And it wasn't clear to me until the other night when I asked if I gave you the baby, what would I get?

And there was no real acceptable answer. But you want your cake and you want to eat it too with no regard for my needs/wants/desires.

My final point is everything was going so well. It baffles me. I mean it could not have been going better. Now, I think everything we've been through would be totally justified if you wanted a baby RIGHT NOW. Today.

But you don't.

You are making the idea of a child our ONLY breaking point as a couple. Otherwise we're perfect. But the truth is there are thousands of reasons why it "might" not work out.

You preemptively broke up with me for some future thing that neither of us are 100% sure that we will even get. That could've been another year, or six months or 5 years to figure that out. You wouldn't take the leap with me. You wanted guarantees and promises... life doesn't work that way.

In the end I just feel bullied. I feel like an ultimatum was presented and there was no way I was going to take it. Not under those circumstances. Never.

I love you. And all things that work with us really work.

I had NO PROBLEMS with our relationship. It was the best thing that's ever happened to me. The only thing I can think of as to why we broke up is you wanted a baby more than you wanted me.

Sun, December 7 at 9:50am

STILL THINKING
ABOUT YOU

Fri, December 12 at 8:57pm

First of all, I know we agreed not to talk anymore.

So please don't be mad at me for texting

Okay

But I did something we said we'd do together and
I feel like I should tell you

No, I feel like it's my duty to tell you

That was a lot of things, what is it?

I know, but what I did involves a big machine

You didn't!

I did

Without me?!!!!

Sorry...

I'm sorry, but I wanted to tell you just in case you ran into me. I know you'd know

I'm speechless

What do you think?

It's perfect

No, it's exquisite.

All thanks to you…

It kills me to know that the next guy will inherit the fruits of my labor

I have to admit, I thought you were nuts this whole time.

I was like he's got a very shallow misguided obsession

But once I started to try on the jeans I was like he's a genius 🥰🥰

Clearly my work is done here

SANTA'S NOT COMING

Thu, December 25 at 11:39am

Merry Christmas!

Merry Christmas!!!!

This would've been our first Christmas together

I know. So sad I'm not with you

I am eating Papa John's with my family and we are dipping it in the garlic butter and were just talking about you

I love that dipping sauce!!!

The best ever and some very good memories.

I have a confession

Ok

I got you a gift

Really?

It's something I got a couple months ago before we...

That's very sweet

I'd like to send it to you

Thank you, that is so thoughtful. But do you think that kind of intimacy is healthy for us?

Probably not

I'm sorry

BUT IF YOU DON'T

Tue, January 6 at 10:01am

Just in Chicago, catching a plane back to LA

Seeing the lake made me think of you

Very sweet of you to say

Not a day goes by that I don't miss and think about you in a hundred different ways

Your text made me burst into tears in the middle of the airport

Being without you is incredibly hard

You are always in my thoughts and close to my heart

I love you. I'll always love you.

I love you too

Just to be clear, my goal wasn't to make you cry. Just wanted you to know how much I think about you.

Your text was so sweet and loving that it made me emotional

You are a wonderful man

Thanks beautiful. Love you

I've been having a really challenging time

I keep doing the math in my head and I know we don't work based on what we want, but I find myself wanting to be with you really, really bad

I'm not sure what either of us can gain from this text, but I'm tired of trying to hide it

I understand. I wish I could make it better but I don't know how to

Has it been as hard for you?

It's been incredibly hard to be without you

You left a huge hole in my heart and life

How does it get better? When?

I pray it gets easier for both of us

But it hasn't

I wish I had the answer. I would tell you

Please tell me when you do.

I will sweet stuff

I just want you to promise me that if you don't want kids that you'll call me. Okay?

And just to be clear if I did want kids there is no other person I would have wanted them with.

You are an amazing woman

It's much bigger than just the kid

Really?! That's news to me. What else is it?

Communication. We've talked about this before.

An openness to have a child is key too

I'm just about to board a plane

If we remove the idea of a child. You're saying our problem was communication?

The relationship we had was the most open and honest relationship I've ever been in.

I'm shocked that that's your reasoning

Have a good flight. Take care and good luck

This is the last you'll hear from me

We talked about how our communication broke down and we worked on it

That being said I don't think it's just a child that keeps us apart

The child is the only reason. Everything else could be worked on

Everything else could be changed or fixed

But I wanted to work with us on the child front

In my eyes we are only not together because of a child

Everything. I mean everything else was a work in progress

This is an insane conversation to have over text while I am about to take off.

If you didn't want a kid, I promise you there is NO reason we would have broken up.

Everything else was doable and workable.

That's as clear as I can say it

Unfortunately it sounds like you think we broke up for other reasons. And that hurts me, deeply b/c that was not clear to me

It was probably a mistake to reach out to you, so I'm sorry

Tue, January 6 at 6:12pm

Just landed

The kid issue is a huge one

I have no idea where life will take me but I know I would have felt resentful if the choice was made for me

That would have been unfair for both of us

I send this with tons of love

THE CHECK IN

Fri, June 10 at 3:33pm

Happy Birthday Zoey!

Thank you!!

You remembered!

Of course!

CHECK YOU BACK

Sun, August 29 at 3:33pm

Happy Birthday!

Awweee, thank you!!!

I THINK I'M OVER YOU

Fri, December 25 at 12:56pm

Merry Christmas!

Same to you! Hope you and your family are well!!

How have you been?

Really well

Can I ask you a random question?

Sure

What did you get me for Christmas last year?

Oh, wow. Really?

I'm sorry. I know I have no right to ask, but I'm dying to know

You know how you're obsessed with Dr. Seuss?

Yeah

I planned a trip for us to go visit the Dr. Seuss Museum in his hometown of Springfield, MA.

And we were going to have tea with Dr. Seuss' wife

Audrey Geisel?!

Yes

My heart just melted

That's the nicest most thoughtful gift someone never gave me.

TEMPTATION

Thu, February 23 at 7:42pm

I'm near your place having a drink with friends...

Can I stop by?

I'm not home at the moment. Is everything okay?

Your place is on my way home

When will you be back?

Call me when you leave

Thu, February 23 at 9:22pm

Leaving now. Are you home?

Is everything ok?

Can we talk on the phone first?

Calling in 2 mins.

Thu, February 23 at 11:34pm

This is what you missed out on...

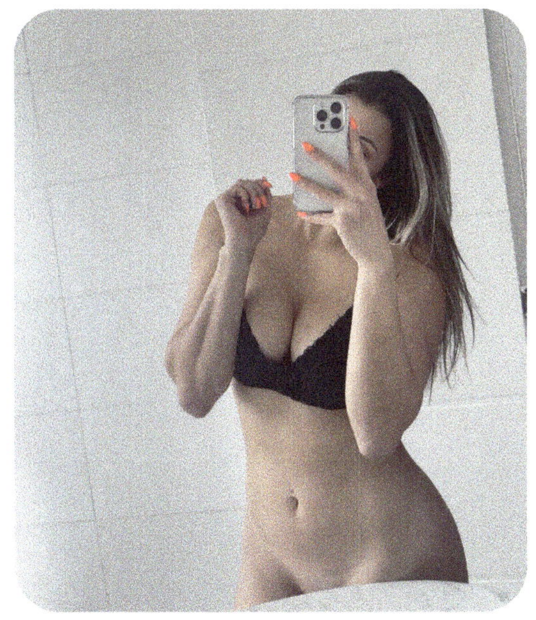

MY THERAPIST SAYS

Tue, March 25 at 5:07pm

I've been thinking about you a lot recently

You've had a starring role in my dreams the last few nights

I was wondering if I could take you to lunch?

I could share my deep thoughts on such topics as the new Drake song or why high waisted pants are a problem for most women's bodies.

I know how you feel about seeing each other and being friends with exs, but I wanted to reach out in case you felt differently now.

And I promise not to try and pressure you into having sex with me again.

I'm still really sorry about my drunken text/call and advancements that night.

BAD IDEA

Wed, March 26 at 3:00pm

Sounds like you've been busy thinking about me...

The only day next week I can meet up would be Tuesday, but in the evening

Let me know

Tuesday night is perfect for me

What part of town is convenient for you?

I'll be coming from the valley but can meet anywhere after 7pm

Let's say 7:30pm. You pick the place

7:30 it is

How about meeting at Farm to Table in Santa Monica?

Perfect.

See you there.

YOU ALWAYS GET WHAT YOU WANT

Tue, April 1 at 3:17pm

I know you already know that agreeing to meet up with you is a very difficult decision for me

After reflecting upon it more I don't feel like anything new will come from it, so I need to cancel

It feels like everything that needed to be said was said the last time we met up.

I really appreciate you and everything I experienced and learned from you. Thank you

But I truly feel like it's time we go our separate ways.

I want nothing but the best for you. You are amazing.

A total catch and you deserve to be happy.

I wasn't going to say this over text as I wanted to wait until I saw you but...

It wanted to bring a different energy around our time together. I'm not coming from a place of pain or the "past stories" and I was hoping you'd do the same.

I wanted to see you as you are now. I wanted to connect from a place of love and compassion.

I'm excited about the possibility of potentially forging new territory together.

I want to focus on the people we've become over the past year and a half and share who we've evolved and grown into with each other.

Even if both of us have changed since we've been together (which we have) what is the reason we'd get together and talk again? Talk about what?

If our last meeting was about closure, what is this about?

Being friends? If so with what purpose?

You are very good at getting what you want, but this time you're going to have to dig deep and tell me clearly and plainly the reason you want to get together.

If you truly are in a new place then you need to tell me what you want to get out of meeting up.

If your intension is just to bring a "different energy" around me that's not enough for me, nor is it specific or forthright enough.

What do you want?

Like I said, I wanted to connect from a new place and specifically not talk about the past.

Just wanted to see what would happen if we gave ourselves a chance to look at each other with fresh eyes, that there might be a chance for us

The idea of possibly dating you again has a lot of joy around it for me

I don't know the new you and I would like to

Thank you. I greatly appreciate all of your honesty

I truly got a lot out of our last talk last year and thought it was rich, insightful and completely necessary.

But to open the door again with you, even if it's from a completely new place, doesn't work for me.

You're clearly in a new place, which makes me very happy, but to try and date again or be friends isn't what I want

It's nothing personal against you, it's just that I've moved on.

And I know for myself that once I've spent that much intimate time with someone, that no matter how much me or that person has changed since, it's very difficult to start anew

Because even though both people are different the slate is never completely clean and clear. We had our moment.

We tried several times to make it work

I want nothing but the best for you.

You are an amazing woman.

But for me, you're the one that got away and our time together has come to an end.

I understand

CRICKETS

Thu, February 13 at 2:21pm

Hello! I can't believe it's been nearly a year since our last text

How are you?

THE STROLLER: TWO YEARS LATER

Sun, November 15 at 1:38pm

So great running into you today!

Your little girl is so incredibly cute!

Thank you!!!! 😬

She looks just like you!

You looked so happy.

I am

That puts a huge smile on my face.

BTW your girlfriend is beautiful
And her jeans fit perfectly 😜

HAHA!!

END OF THREAD